This book belongs to:

....

....

....

Age ....

BYE BABY BUNTING
and other rhymes

Bye, baby bunting,
Daddy's gone a-hunting,
Gone to get a rabbit skin,
To wrap the baby bunting in.

Old Farmer Giles
Walked seven miles
With his faithful dog, old Rover;
And old Farmer Giles
When he came to the stiles,
Took a run, and jumped clean over.

Little Poll Parrot
Sat in his garret
Eating toast and tea;
A little brown mouse
Jumped into the house,
And stole it all away.

I do not like thee, Doctor Fell,
The reason why I cannot tell;
But this I know, and know full well,
I do not like thee, Doctor Fell.

NASTY MEDICINE

VERY NASTY MEDICINE

Insey Winsey spider,
Climbed up the water spout;
Down came the rain
And washed the spider out;
Out came the sunshine
And dried up all the rain;
Insey Winsey spider,
Climbed up the spout again.

Bulls head

"Who goes there?"
"A Grenadier."
"What do you want?"
"A pot of beer?"

Cuckoo, cuckoo, what do you do?
In April I open my bill;
In May I sing night and day;
In June I change my tune;
In July I prepare to fly;
In August away I must.

Terence McDiddler
The three-stringed fiddler
Can charm, if you please,
The fish from the seas.

There was a man and he had nought
And robbers came to rob him;
He crept up to the chimney pot,
And then they thought they had him.

But he got down on the other side,
And then they could not find him;
He ran fourteen miles in fifteen days,
And never looked behind him.

Dame Trot and her cat
Sat down to chat;
The Dame sat on this side
And puss sat on that.

"Puss," says the Dame,
"Can you catch a rat
Or a mouse in the dark?"
«Purr!" says the cat.

Davy Davy Dumpling,
Boil him in a pot;
Sugar him and butter him;
And eat him while he's hot.

Elsie Marley is grown so fine,
She won't get up to feed the swine,
But lies in bed till eight or nine,
Lazy Elsie Marley.

My mother said, I never should
Play with the gypsies in the wood.
If I did, then she would say:
Naughty girl to disobey.

A was an Apple Pie

B
Bit it

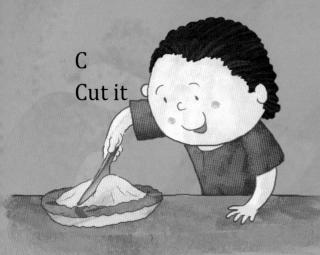

C
Cut it

D
Dealt it

E
Eat it

F
Fought it

G
Got it

H
Had it

I
Inspected it

J Jumped
for it

K
Kept it

L Longed
for it

M
Mourned
for it

N
Nodded
at it

O
Opened it

P
Peeped in it

Q
Quartered it

R
Ran for it

S
Stole it

T
Took it

U
Upset it

V
Viewed it

W
Wanted it

XYZ
All wished for a piece in their hand

Hector Protector was dressed all in green;
Hector Protector was sent to the Queen.
The Queen did not like him,
No more did the King;
So Hector Protector was sent back again.

19

Gregory Griggs, Gregory Griggs,
Had twenty-seven different wigs.
He wore them up, he wore them down,
To please the people of the town;
He wore them east, he wore them west,
But he never could tell which he loved the best.

I am his Highness's dog at Kew;
Pray, tell me sir, whose dog are you?

Bat, bat, come under my hat,
And I'll give you a slice of bacon;
And when I bake, I'll give you a cake,
If I am not mistaken.

Molly, my sister, and I fell out,
And what do you think it was all about?
She loved coffee and I loved tea,
And that was the reason we could not agree.

Four and twenty tailors
Went to catch a snail;
The bravest one amongst them
Dared not touch her tail.
She put out her horns,
Like a little Kyloe cow.
Run, tailors, run,
She'll have you all even now!

23

I had a little hen,
The prettiest ever seen;
She washed up the dishes,
And kept the house clean,

She went to the mill
To fetch me some flour,
And always got home
In less than an hour.

Little maid, pretty maid, whither goest thou?
Down in the meadow to milk my cow.
Shall I go with thee? No, not now;
When I send for thee, then come thou.

She baked me my bread,
She brewed me my ale,

She sat by the fire
And told a fine tale.

A wise old owl sat in an oak,
The more he heard the less he spoke;
The less he spoke the more he heard.
Why aren't we all like that wise old bird?

Little Miss Muffet
Sat on her tuffet,
Eating her curds and whey;
There came a big spider,
Who sat down beside her
And frightened Miss Muffet away.

LITTLE BO-PEEP
and other rhymes

Little Bo-peep has lost her sheep,
And can't tell where to find them;
Leave them alone, and they'll come home,
Bringing their tails behind them.

Jack and Jill.
Went up the hill,
To fetch a pail of water;

Jack fell down,
And broke his crown,
And Jill came tumbling after.

I love little pussy,
Her coat is so warm,
And if I don't hurt her,
She'll do me no harm.
So I'll not pull her tail,
Or drive her away,
But Pussy and I
Very gently will play.
She will sit by my side,
And I'll give her some food,
And she'll like me because
I am gentle and good.

Doctor Foster went to Gloucester
In a shower of rain;
He stepped in a puddle,
Right up to his middle,
And never went there again.

Girls and boys come out to play,
The moon doth shine as bright as day.
Leave your supper and leave your sleep,
And come with your playfellows into the street.
Come with a whoop and come with a call,
Come with a good will or not at all.
Up the ladder and down the wall,
A half-penny loaf will serve us all;
You find milk, and I'll find flour,
And we'll have a pudding in half an hour.

The Man in the Moon
Looked out of the moon,
Looked out of the moon and said,
"This time for all children on the earth
To think about getting to bed!"

Fee, fi, fo, fum,
I smell the blood of
an Englishman:
Be he alive or be he
dead,
I'll grind his bones
to make my bread.

Here am I,
little Jumping Joan,
When I'm by myself,
I'm all alone.

Hark, hark, the dogs do bark,
The beggars are coming to town;
Some in rags and some in jags,
And one in a velvet gown.

Ring-a-ring o'roses,
A pocket full of posies,
A-tishoo! A-tishoo!
We all fall down.

Charley Parley stole the barley
Out of the baker's shop.
The baker came out,
and gave him a clout,
Which made poor Charley hop.

There was an old woman who lived in a shoe;
She had so many children she didn't know what to do.
She gave them some broth without any bread;
Then whipped them all soundly and put them to bed.

One, two,
Buckle my shoe;

Three, four,
Knock at the door;

Five, six,
Pick up sticks;

Seven, eight,
Lay them straight;

Nine, ten
A big fat hen;

Eleven, twelve,
Dig and delve;

Thirteen, fourteen,
Maids a-courting;

Fifteen, sixteen,
Maids in the kitchen;

Seventeen, eighteen,
Maids a-waiting;

Nineteen, twenty,
My plate's empty.

Rock-a-bye, baby, on the tree-top.
When the wind blows
The cradle will rock;

When the bough breaks,
The cradle will fall,
Down will come baby,
Cradle and all.

Heeper-peeper, chimney
sweeper,
Had a wife and couldn't
keep her.
Had another, didn't love her,
Up the chimney he did
shove her.

Please to remember
The fifth of November,
Gunpowder treason and plot;
I see no reason
Why gunpowder treason
Should ever be forgot.

Penny
for the
GUY

41

Mary, Mary, quite contrary,
How does your garden grow?
With silver bells and cockle shells,
And pretty maids all in a row.

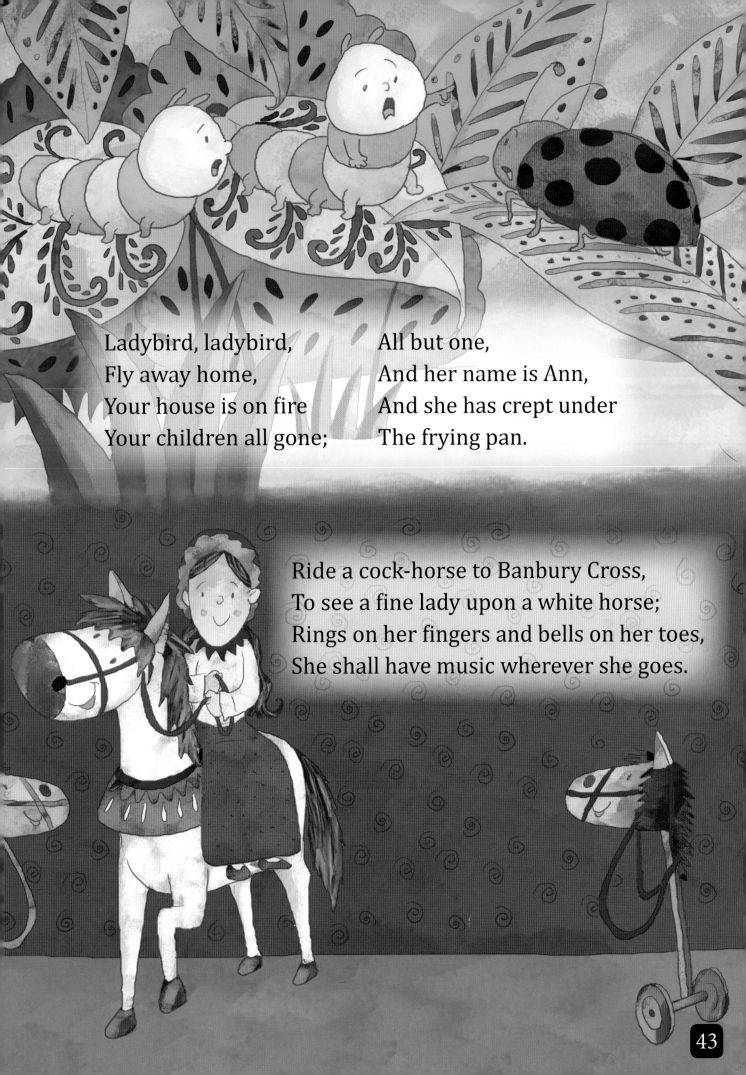

Ladybird, ladybird,
Fly away home,
Your house is on fire
Your children all gone;

All but one,
And her name is Ann,
And she has crept under
The frying pan.

Ride a cock-horse to Banbury Cross,
To see a fine lady upon a white horse;
Rings on her fingers and bells on her toes,
She shall have music wherever she goes.

Hey diddle, diddle,
The cat and the fiddle,
The cow jumped over the
moon;
The little dog laughed
To see such sport,
And the dish ran away
with the spoon.

There was a crooked man,
And he walked a crooked mile,
He found a crooked sixpence
Against a crooked stile;
He bought a crooked cat,
Which caught a crooked mouse,
And they all lived together
In a little crooked house.

Christmas is coming,
The geese are getting fat,
Please to put a penny
In the old man's hat
If you haven't got a penny,
A ha'penny will do;
If you haven't got a ha'penny,
Then God bless you!

Little Polly Flinders
Sat amongst the cinders,
Warming her pretty little toes;
Her mother came and caught her,
And whipped her little daughter
For spoiling her nice new clothes.

How many miles to Babylon?
Three-score miles and ten.
Can I get there by candle-light?
Yes, and back again.
If your heels and nimble and light,
You may get there by candle-light.

Up the wooden hill
To Bedfordshire,
Down Sheet Lane,
To Blanket Fair.

Polly put the kettle on,
Polly put the kettle on,
Polly put the kettle on,
We'll all have tea.
Sukey take it off again,
Sukey take it off again,
Sukey take it off again,
They've all gone away.

It's raining, it's pouring,
The old man's snoring;
He got into bed
And bumped his head
And couldn't get up in the morning.

49

THE GRAND OLD DUKE OF YORK
and other rhymes

Oh, the grand old Duke of York,

He had ten thousand men;

He marched them up to the top of the hill,

And he marched them down again.

And when they were up, they were up,

And when they were down, they were down.

And when they were only halfway up,

They were neither up nor down.

There was a crow
Sat on a stone
When he was gone,
then there was none.

King Pippin built a fine new hall,
Pastry and piecrust were the wall,
Windows made of black pudding and white
Slates were pancakes- you never saw the like.

There were once two cats of Kilkenny
Each thought there was one cat too many;
So they fought and they fit;
And they scratched and they bit,
Till, excepting their nails,
And the tips of their tails,
Instead of two cats, there weren't any.

Here's Sulky Sue!
What shall we do?
Put her in the corner,
Till she comes to.

This old man, he played one,
He played Nick Nack, on my drum!
Nick Nack Paddy Whack!
Give a dog a bone,
This old man came rolling home.

On Saturday night I lost my wife,
And where do you think I found her? "
Up in the moon, singing a tune,
And all the stars around her.

There was a little man,
And he had a little gun,
And his bullets were made
of lead, lead, lead;
He saw a little duck,
Upon a little brook,
And he shot it right through
the head, head, head.

Hush, little baby, don't say a word,
Papa's going to buy you a mocking bird.

If the mocking bird
won't sing,
Papa's going to buy
you a diamond ring.

If the diamond ring turns to brass,
Papa's going to buy you a looking glass.

If that looking glass gets broke,
Papa's going to buy you a billy goat.

If that billy goat runs away,
Papa's going to buy you another today.

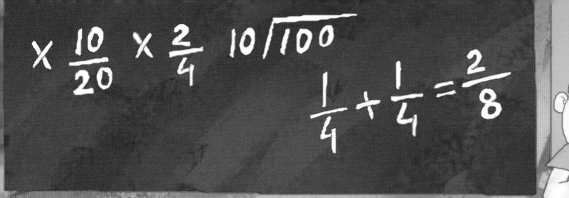

Multiplication is vexation,
Division is as bad;
The Rule of Three perplexes me,
And fractions drive me mad.

If all the world were paper
And all the seas were ink;
And all the trees were bread and cheese,
What should we have to drink?

I saw a Bee sat on a wall,
It said, "Buzz," and that was all!

Hannah Bantry,
In the pantry,
Gnawing at a mutton bone;
How she gnawed it,
How she clawed it
When she found herself alone.

There was a jolly miller once
Lived on the river Dee;
He worked and sang from morn
till night,
No lark more blithe than he.
And this the burden of his song
Forever used to be,
I care for nobody, no, not I,
And nobody cares for me.

When the wind is in the East,
This neither good for man nor beast;

When the wind is in the North
The skilful fisher goes not forth;

When the wind is in the South,
It blows the bait in the fishes' mouth;

When the wind is in the West,
Then 'tis at the very best.

What are little girls made of?
Sugar and spice,
And all things nice.
What are little boys made of?
Snips and snails,
And puppy-dog tails.

Queen, Queen Caroline
Washed her hair in turpentine,
Turpentine to make it shine,
Queen, Queen Caroline

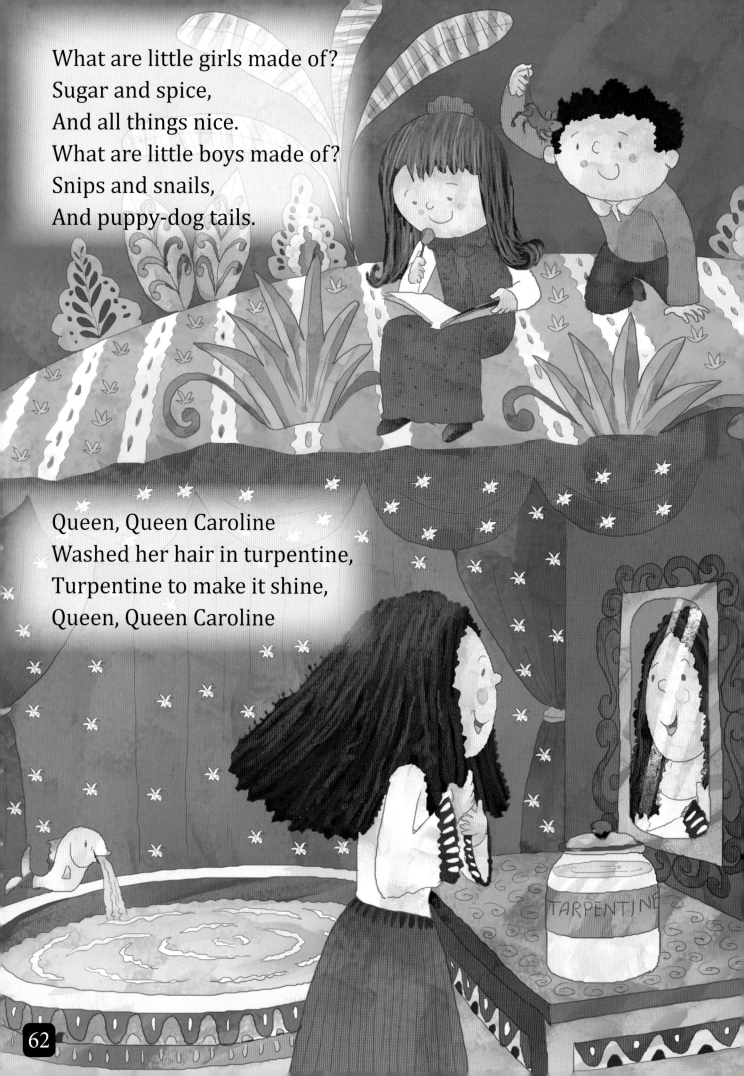

There was a rat, for
want of stairs,
Went down a rope to
say his prayers.

Shoe the horse, shoe the horse,
Shoe the bay mare.
Here a nail, there a nail,
Still, she stands there.

63

Magpie, magpie, flutter and flee,
Turn up your tail and good luck come to me.
One for sorrow, two for joy,
Three for a girl, four for a boy,
Five for silver; six for gold,
Seven for a secret ne'er to he told.

My father died a month ago
And left me all his riches;
A feather bed, a wooden leg,
And a pair of leather breeches;
A coffee pot without a spout,
A cup without a handle,
A tobacco pipe without a lid,
And half a farthing candle.

Little Nancy Etticoat
In a white petticoat,
The longer she stands
The shorter she grows.

Three young rats with black felt hats,

Three young ducks with new straw flats,

Three young dogs with curling tails,

Three young cats with demi-veils,

Went out to walk with two young pigs
In satin vests and sorrel wigs;

But suddenly it chanced to rain
And so they all went home again.

Into the basin put the plums,
Stirabout, stirabout, stirabout!
Next the good white flour comes,
Stirabout, stirabout, stirabout!
Sugar and peel and eggs and spice,
Stirabout, stirabout, stirabout!
Mix them and fix them and cook them twice,
Stirabout, stirabout, stirabout!

Warm hands, warm hands,
The men are gone to plough.
If you want to warm your hands,
Warm your hands now.

Barber, barber, shave a pig,
How many hairs to make a wig?
Four and twenty, that's enough,
Give the barber a pinch of snuff.

Oh where, oh where has my little dog gone?
Oh where, oh where can he be?
With his ears cut short and his tail cut long,
Oh where, oh where is he?

Good night,
Sleep tight,
Wake up bright
In the morning light,
To do what's right
With all your might.

Hickory, dickory, dock,
The mouse ran up the clock.
The clock struck one,
The mouse ran down,
Hickory, dickory, dock.

Jack be nimble,
Jack be quick,
Jack jump over
The candlestick.

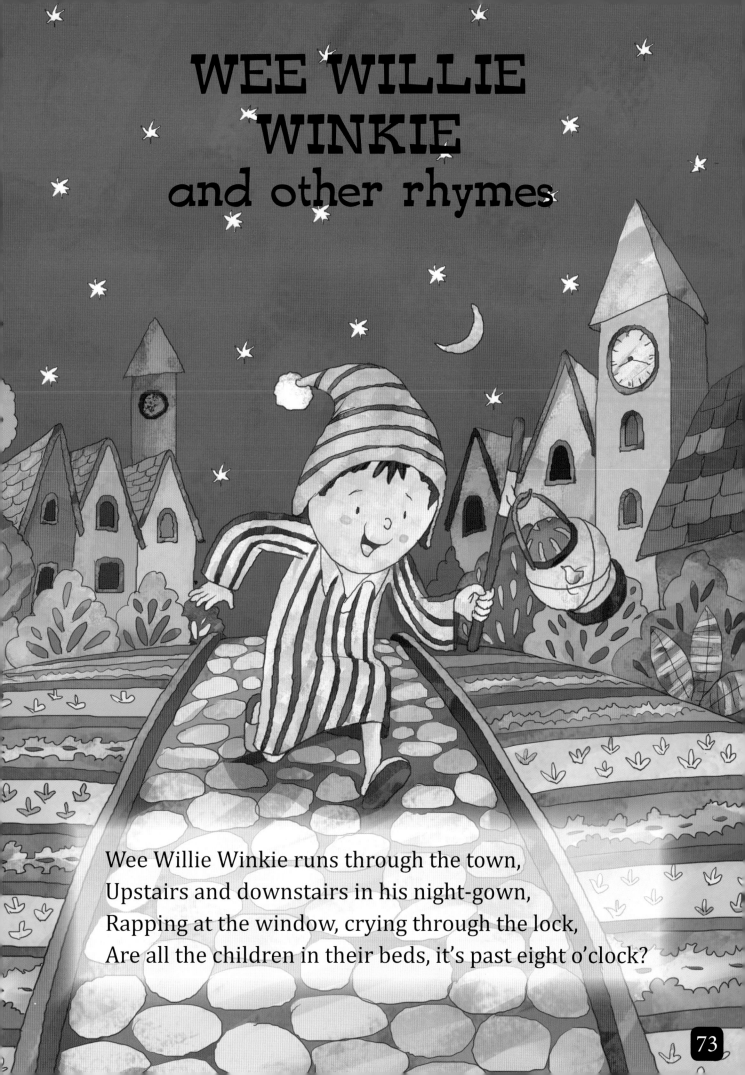

WEE WILLIE WINKIE

and other rhymes

Wee Willie Winkie runs through the town,
Upstairs and downstairs in his night-gown,
Rapping at the window, crying through the lock,
Are all the children in their beds, it's past eight o'clock?

Lavender's blue, dilly, dilly,
Lavender's green,
When I am king, dilly, dilly,
You shall be queen.

Jack Sprat could eat no fat,
His wife could eat no lean,
And so between them both, you see,
They licked the platter clean.

Six little mice sat down to spin;
Pussy passed by and she peeped in.
What are you doing, my little men?
Weaving coats for gentlemen.
Shall I come in and cut off your threads?
No, no, Mistress Pussy, you'd bite off our heads.
Oh, no, I'll not; I'll help you to spin.
That may be so, but you don't come in.

75

Cock a doodle doo!
My dame has lost her shoe,
My master's lost his fiddling stick
And knows not what to do.
Cock a doodle doo!
What is my dame to do?
Till master finds his fiddling stick
She'll dance without her shoe.

Tom, Tom, the piper's son,
Stole a pig and away did run;
The pig was eat,
And Tom was beat,
And Tom went howling
Down the street.

Roses are red,
Violets are blue,

Sugar is sweet
And so are you.

There was an old woman
Lived under a hill,
And if she's not gone
She lives there still.

Punch and Judy
Fought for a pie;
Punch gave Judy
A knock in the eye.
Says Punch to Judy,
'Will you have any more?'
Says Judy to Punch,
'My eye is too sore.'

Hickety, pickety, my black hen,
She lays eggs for gentlemen;
Sometimes nine, and sometimes ten,
Hickety, pickety, my black hen.

The north wind doth blow,
And we shall have snow,
And what will poor Robin do then,
Poor thing?
He'll sit in a barn,
And keep himself warm,
And hide his head under his wing,
Poor thing.

Monday

Tuesday

Wednesday

Monday's child is fair of face,
Tuesday's child is full of grace,
Wednesday's child is full of woe,
Thursday's child has far to go,
Friday's child is loving and giving,
Saturday's child works hard for its living,
And the child that's born on the Sabbath day
Is bonny and blithe, and good and gay.

Thursday

Friday

Saturday

Sunday

Old Mother Hubbard
Went to her cupboard,
To fetch her poor dog a bone;
But when she got there
The cupboard was bare
And so the poor dog had none.

She went to the baker's
To buy him some bread;
But when she came back
The poor dog was dead.

She went to the joiner's
To buy him a coffin.
But when she came back
The poor dog was laughing.

She took a clean dish
To get him some tripe;
But when she came back
He was smoking a pipe.

She went to the fishmonger's
To buy him some fish;
But when she came back
He was licking the dish.

She went to the tavern
For white wine and red;
But when she came back
The dog stood on his head.

She went to the fruiterer's
To buy him some fruit;
But when she came back
He was playing the flute.

She went to the tailor's
To buy him a coat;
But when she came back
He was riding a goat.

She went to the hatter's
To buy him a hat;
But when she came back
He was feeding the cat.

83

She went to the barber's
To buy him a wig;
But when she came back
He was dancing a jig.

She went to the cobbler's
To buy him some shoes;
But when she came back
He was reading the news.

She went to the seamstress
To buy him some linen;
But when she came back
The dog was a-spinning.

She went to the hosier's
To buy him some hose;
But when she came back
He was dressed in his clothes.

The dame made a curtsey,
The dog made a bow;
The dame said, 'Your servant,'
The dog said, 'Bow-wow.'

Little Tommy Tucker
Sings for his supper,
What shall we give him?
White bread and butter.
How shall he cut it
Without e'er a knife?
How shall he marry
Without e'er a wife?

Lucy Locket lost her pocket,
Kitty Fisher found it;
Not a penny was there in it,
Only ribbon round it.

The Lion and the Unicorn
were fighting for the crown,
The Lion beat the Unicorn
all round the town.
Some gave them white bread
and some gave them brown,
And some gave them plum cake,
and drummed them out of town.

Red sky at night,
Shepherd's delight;
Red sky in the morning,
Shepherd's warning.

Two little dicky birds
Sat upon a wall,
One called Peter,
One called Paul.

Fly away Peter,
Fly away Paul;
Come back Peter,
Come back Paul.

Peter Piper picked a peck
of pickled pepper;
A peck of pickled pepper
Peter Piper picked.
If Peter Piper picked a peck
of pickled pepper,
Where's the peck of pickled pepper
Peter Piper picked?

87

Here we go round the mulberry bush,
The mulberry bush, the mulberry bush,
Here we go round the mulberry bush,
On a cold and frosty morning.

I see the moon
And the moon sees me;
God bless the moon,
And God bless me.

See-saw, Margery Daw,
Johnny shall have a new master;
He shall have but a penny a day,
Because he can't work any faster.

89

Ding, dong, bell,
Pussy's in the well.
Who put her in?
Little Johnny Green.

Who pulled her out?
Little Tommy Stout.
What a naughty boy was that
To try to drown poor pussy cat,
Who never did him any harm,
But killed the mice in his father's barn.

Twinkle, twinkle, little star,
How I wonder what you are!
Up above the world so high,
Like a diamond in the sky.

Humpty Dumpty sat on a wall,
Humpty Dumpty had a great fall;
All the King's horses,
And all the King's men,
Couldn't put Humpty together again .

A diller, a dollar,
A ten o'clock scholar,
What makes you come so soon?
You used to come at ten o'clock,
But now you come at noon.

Pat-a-cake, pat-a-
cake, baker's man,
Bake me a cake as
fast as you can;
Pat it and prick it,
and mark it with B,
Put it in the oven for
Baby and me.

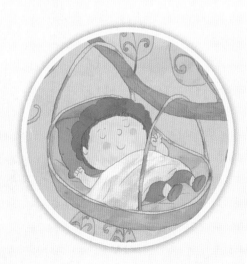